Agatha

Girl of Mystery

GROSSET & DUNLAP
Penguin Young Readers Group
An Imprint of Penguin Random House LLC

Original Title: Agatha Mistery: Intrigo a Hollywood
Text by Sir Steve Stevenson
Original cover and illustrations by Stefano Turconi

English language edition copyright © 2015 Penguin Random House LLC. Original edition published by Istituto Geografico De Agostini S.p.A., Italy, 2012 © 2012 Atlantyca Dreamfarm s.r.l., Italy

International Rights © Atlantyca S.p.A.—via Leopardi 8, 20123 Milano, Italia
foreignrights@atlantyca.it—www.atlantyca.com

Published in 2015 by Grosset & Dunlap, an imprint of Penguin Random House LLC, 345 Hudson Street, New York, New York 10014. GROSSET & DUNLAP is a trademark of Penguin Random House LLC. Printed in the USA.

Library of Congress Cataloging-in-Publication Data is available.

10 9 8 7 6 5 4 3 2 1

ISBN 978-0-448-48680-2

Agatha

Girl of Mystery

The Hollywood Intrigue

by Sir Steve Stevenson
illustrated by Stefano Turconi

translated by Siobhan Tracey
adapted by Maya Gold

Grosset & Dunlap
An Imprint of Penguin Random House

NINTH MISSION
Agents

Agatha
Twelve years old, an aspiring mystery writer; has a formidable memory

Dash
Agatha's cousin and student at the private school Eye International Detective Academy

Chandler
Butler and former boxer with impeccable British style

Watson
Obnoxious Siberian cat with the nose of a bloodhound

Uncle Bud
Retired NASCAR champion, who now works part-time as a Hollywood stuntman

DESTINATION

Hollywood, California

Hollywood

OBJECTIVE

Navigate the behind-the-scenes dramas of a Hollywood movie studio and find out who is trying to sabotage the film *Fatal Error*

The Investigation Begins...

$\mathcal{D}$ashiell Mistery was fried. While all his friends were hanging out in London parks, enjoying their freedom from school, his summer vacation had not even begun. In fact, Dash was starting to think this might be the year when he wouldn't get any vacation at all. Ever since he had enrolled at the prestigious Eye International Detective Academy, he'd been sent all over the world on daredevil investigations.

This time, though, his exhaustion was not the result of a top secret mission. A lanky, lazy teenage boy who loved staying up late, Dash didn't have a clue what he was getting himself

into when he signed up for a summer martial-arts class offered by his school.

On this Saturday morning, his muscles felt like dough. Even his bones ached. Dash dragged his stiff legs out of bed, microwaved three chocolate-chip pancakes, and shoveled them into his mouth. Then he hoisted his backpack onto his shoulder and left his mom's penthouse apartment at Baker Palace. It was still early, and the city sidewalks were almost deserted. Dash trudged to the nearest Tube station and sprawled across two empty seats on the short ride to his destination.

The martial-arts dojo was right in the center of London, neatly hidden among tall brick buildings. Dash knocked on a large wooden door decorated with Asian calligraphy. An ancient Japanese man swung it open. He had white hair and a drooping mustache, and was wrapped in a monk's cloak.

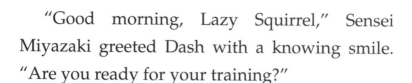

"Good morning, Lazy Squirrel," Sensei Miyazaki greeted Dash with a knowing smile. "Are you ready for your training?"

Dash grunted. Snarling, he crossed the Zen garden to the wooden pagoda where classes were held. *Lazy Squirrel? What a ridiculous name!* Not to mention the cheesy metaphors his teacher was always using to explain martial-arts basics. Dash had signed up for the class because he'd always dreamed of inflicting lightning-fast strikes like Bruce Lee, coolly dodging bad guys like James Bond, and launching himself into acrobatic moves like the heroes of *The Matrix*. But through all the weeks of exercise, he hadn't learned anything even close to that cool.

While Sensei Miyazaki waited under the pagoda with his arms folded, Dash pulled his white uniform *gi* from his backpack, slowly put it on, and walked barefoot to a large stone in the middle of the garden.

"Ready when you are, Professor . . . um, Sensei," he mumbled. "Same deal, right? I have to . . . what, free my monkey mind from negative thoughts?"

"Black clouds always bring on a storm," the old monk intoned. Then he rotated his palms in the air, closed his eyes, and tilted his chin upward. "Now, breathe . . . breathe . . . ," he said.

"How long do I have to . . . um . . . breathe, breathe?" Dash asked, gulping oxygen.

"Until your skies are calm, Lazy Squirrel," the teacher replied. Then he disappeared inside the pagoda.

The young detective spent the next few hours sitting cross-legged on the stone. Zen meditation wasn't really his thing; instead of calming him down, it made a million questions career through his head. Was Sensei Miyazaki really an Eye International agent? And if so, why wasn't he teaching Dash how to fight bad guys, defend

himself with his bare hands, and do cool flying kicks? And the most pressing question of all: *When was lunch?*

He didn't realize he had dozed off until a sudden snap of fingers woke him at noon.

"I didn't do it!" Dash jolted awake. "What's up?"

The elderly monk stood in front of him, calmly crunching a sesame cracker. "Time for your first test of the day," he announced. "This ancient technique is called the Twisted Eel."

"What?" Dash protested, standing abruptly. "Don't I get a lunch break?"

Sensei Miyazaki's mustache quivered in disappointment. "This isn't a restaurant, Lazy Squirrel," he said stiffly. "You're here to learn"— *crunch, crunch*—"not to gorge yourself."

Dash's stomach was growling, but he obeyed the teacher. The only way to get out of here as soon as possible was to satisfy his demands. But when

Dash stepped around the corner of the pagoda, he was stunned. The whole space was filled with a forest of ropes lashed to sturdy bamboo poles. The ropes were stretched at various heights and angles, tied close together like a giant web. "What is all this?" he asked, alarmed.

Miyazaki's lips stretched into a mocking grin. "To free yourself from your adversaries, you must learn to slip from their grasp like an eel," he replied, raising one finger. "Make your way to the far side without ever touching a rope . . . if you can!"

Dash cracked his knuckles, determined. He would prove his worth by passing this test without a hitch! He avoided the first rope by tilting his head sharply, then pivoted on his toes over the second. He flexed his thin shoulders backward and slid under the third as if doing the limbo. "Piece of cake!" he exclaimed, jumping over the next.

As he gloated, Dash heard a loud trill coming from the backpack he'd left near the meditation stone. Inside its front pocket was the precious multifunction device he used for school: a state-of-the-art high-tech gadget known as the EyeNet.

The insistent ringing could only mean one thing: He'd been assigned a new mission!

Momentarily distracted by that thought, Dash tripped over a rope. He pitched forward a few feet and landed, half-dangling from a dense tangle of ropes, facedown in the grass. With a mouthful of dirt, he didn't even say "Ouch!"

"Are you hurt, Lazy Squirrel?" Miyazaki sounded concerned.

A hand shot out from the tangle of knots. "Sensei, please pass me my phone!" exclaimed Dash. Noting the monk's hesitation, he added in a whisper, "It's my EyeNet. Must be something urgent!"

When Miyazaki handed him the titanium

device, Dash checked the message on-screen, and his eyes widened. Without realizing it, he managed to extricate himself from the ropes in a single smooth move.

"Hollywood . . . ?" he muttered, running a hand through his hair. "Are they out of their minds?"

Amazed at the skill with which his young student had freed himself, Sensei Miyazaki stood speechless as Dash took off like a flash. Before the teacher could even congratulate him, he had disappeared into the London streets.

Of course, Dash had rushed off to get help from his genius cousin Agatha Mistery.

An Unforgettable Anniversary

cMistery House was a bright spot of color in an otherwise gray London suburb. Today, the lavender-roofed Victorian mansion had a sparkling air of celebration. In the luxuriant gardens, fountains gushed among blooming rhododendrons, while classical music spilled out from the house. It was just the right atmosphere to celebrate the twelfth-year anniversary of indefatigable jack-of-all-trades Chandler at Mistery House.

"Such a shame Mom and Dad got held up in Tasmania," said Agatha, casting a disappointed gaze at the impeccably set table, loaded with

goodies. "It would have been perfect if they were here, too."

"They'll be home soon enough, Miss," replied the impassive butler as he settled into a chair. The former heavyweight boxer's bulk provoked a loud creak, but the chair held his weight. "I'm very grateful for all this attention," he added softly, his voice betraying emotion.

Agatha tapped the tip of her small, upturned nose with one finger, an unmistakable sign that she was pondering something. "Do you know what my parents are doing down there?" she asked, her eyes shining.

"I'm so sorry, Miss." Chandler shook his head gravely. "I have absolutely no idea."

"Before they left London, Mom mentioned they wanted to study a rare local species," said Agatha, passing him a silver platter of oysters. "Try to guess which one!"

"The famous Tasmanian devil?" the butler

guessed. He swallowed a tasty lemon-and-parsley-sprinkled oyster in one gulp. Agatha had ordered all of his favorite foods for this anniversary luncheon.

"The largest carnivorous marsupial in the world? No, too obvious!" Agatha laughed. "You won't believe it, but they're studying some slimy green frogs that live only in sulfurous jungle swamps . . ."

"Slimy frogs? Sulfurous swamps?" Chandler echoed. He lowered his gaze to the briny shellfish on the platter, suddenly losing his appetite.

Struggling to maintain his usual calm, he asked, "What's so special about these frogs?"

Agatha pulled her leather-bound notebook from her back pocket. She always kept it with her in case she needed

to record any detail of a topic that tickled her fancy. Like all members of the Mistery family, Agatha had chosen to pursue an unusual career. She wanted to be a world-famous mystery writer and was always taking notes for her stories.

"I've consulted some of the scientific magazines in the library over the past few days," she explained, flicking through the pages. "It seems that this particular species has a gland that possesses miraculous medicinal properties."

"How extraordinary," Chandler said politely.

He was very familiar with his young mistress's talents: an incomparable memory, dazzling intuition, attention to detail, and many other qualities that made her a decidedly out-of-the-ordinary twelve-year-old girl.

"But what am I thinking? Our lovely lunch will get cold." Agatha excused herself, put her notebook away, and grabbed a seafood skewer. "You know what?" she said, beaming. "I'm glad

to be celebrating this anniversary with you and our darling cat, Watson. You're the best friends anybody could have!"

"Aren't you forgetting somebody, Miss?"

Agatha looked amused. "You mean my dear cousin Dash?" she asked, twirling the skewer playfully. "I invited him, too, but he said it was a bad time. He's enrolled in some crazy martial-arts course and needs to practice all day. But I bet he'll drop in to say hello before the end of the day. He won't want to miss a slice of your—"

Agatha stopped in mid-sentence, covering her mouth with her hand. "Ooops . . . I'm such a loudmouth!" She blushed. "I nearly ruined the surprise!"

The butler raised an eyebrow, pretending that he knew nothing. That morning, he had spotted a five-layer Sacher torte on a platter in the pantry. The delicious Viennese chocolate-and-apricot layer cake was his favorite dessert.

Agatha quickly changed the subject, and as soon as they'd finished their lunch, she asked Chandler to close his eyes and wait for her to bring his surprise gift to the table.

That was the moment when everything stopped being perfect.

"Watson!" Agatha cried in despair as she entered the pantry. "What have you done?"

Chandler turned off the opera CD they'd been playing and peeked through the partially open door. Attracted by the delicious aroma, the white Siberian cat had climbed on top of the cake, spreading whipped cream all over the counter. Now he was cleaning chocolate and apricot jam from his fur as though nothing had happened.

"Why couldn't you raid the leftover fish like a normal cat?" Agatha scolded. Grabbing a bar of soap, she turned on the sink and thrust the cat under running water. Watson yowled as splashes and bubbles flew everywhere. "You're such a

bad boy!" Agatha told him, unable to suppress a smile. "Stop complaining, you need a good scrub."

As if bathing a furious cat weren't chaotic enough, the doorbell rang. Chandler got up to check the security camera on the front gate and saw a police officer holding a figure in what looked like loose white pajamas. As Chandler went to tell Agatha, Watson leapt out of the sink and ran upstairs, leaving a trail of wet paw prints.

"The police?" Agatha sounded confused.

"That's right, Miss," the butler confirmed. "And some oddball in a white kimono. He looks a lot like—"

Agatha burst out laughing and strode to the video-intercom. "Now it all makes perfect sense! Our dear Dash has arrived a bit early!" Pressing a button, Agatha spoke to the officer to reassure him. "Don't worry, that really is my cousin," she explained. "I'm guessing he forgot his keys . . ."

"That's right," said Dash. "I tried ringing the doorbell, but nobody answered. So I thought I'd climb over the wall . . ."

"Bad idea," the officer said. "I received a report that some sort of ninja was trying to break into Mistery House, but he kept falling down . . ."

Embarrassed, Dash stared at his feet. To spare him more awkwardness, Agatha buzzed the gate open. "It's all okay," she told the policeman. "We had loud music playing and must not have heard

him ring the doorbell. It's our fault. Thank you, officer."

Dash winked at the security camera and sped up the driveway. Agatha and Chandler met him on the marble stairs, eager to find out what was so urgent.

"We've got to go!" Dash exclaimed. "We take off in two hours from Heathrow Airport!"

"And where are we going?" asked Agatha, smiling at her cousin's uniform. "Some remote martial-arts temple in Tibet?"

Even Chandler's stiff upper lip twitched a bit at her joke.

"Cousin . . ."—*pant, pant*—". . . check this out . . ." Dash bent his knees, catching his breath as Agatha read the text on his EyeNet. "At nine o'clock tonight, we have an appointment with Robert Royce . . ."

"The Hollywood producer?" Chandler, a movie fan, looked astonished.

"If memory serves me correctly, the location indicated in this message is a neighborhood known as Century City." Agatha peered at the EyeNet, then pushed her hair behind her ears and added, "The metropolitan area of Los Angeles is huge. We'll need Uncle Bud's help so we don't get lost on the freeways."

"Uncle Bud?" Dash said in surprise. "Who's that?"

He and Chandler stood in stunned silence as Agatha turned on her heel and went back in the house.

Dash ran after her, spitting out questions. "Who's Uncle Bud? Does he live in LA? Is he marked on your map?"

He was, of course, referring to the globe on which Agatha noted all the contact details and information about members of the vast Mistery clan, who were scattered all over the planet.

"Uncle Bud and I correspond often," she said

calmly, toweling off Watson's fur. "He used to be a champion race-car driver, but now he works as a rare-car mechanic and sometimes as a stuntman for Hollywood films."

Dash scratched his cheek nervously. "A stuntman?"

"You know the action scenes in movies where they have car chases, with spectacular stunts and incredible crashes? Bud stands in for the actors during the most daring parts!"

"He won't be too reckless, will he?" Dash sounded nervous.

"Of course not. Stunt drivers have to have perfect control, or they wouldn't be able to do their job safely. Now, we're in a hurry, right? Go change your clothes and download the case files. I'll do the rest!"

Faced with such confidence, Dash fell silent. These investigations always made him sweat, and he didn't want his professors to find out

that his brilliant cousin played such a big part in all of his triumphs. Agatha was already placing a phone call to Uncle Bud, so Dash took a deep breath—*breathe, breathe, Lazy Squirrel*—and got ready to leave.

Fifteen minutes later, they all met by the fountain. Watson smelled like lavender soap and was strutting inside his cat carrier. Agatha wore a flowered dress and a wide-brimmed sun hat. Chandler, in his elegant navy tuxedo, loaded their luggage into the limousine's trunk without batting an eyelash.

When the butler held open the passenger door, Dash suddenly remembered that today was Chandler's anniversary. "Oh no," he stuttered apologetically. "I hope I haven't ruined your celebration. I'll make it up to you, I promise . . ."

Agatha gave him a reassuring smile. "Don't worry, Dash," she laughed. "The dessert course has just been postponed!"

Cast of Characters

During the long flight to Los Angeles, the three companions pored over the EyeNet files. They soon discovered that, as usual, the school had only sent the bare bones of information about the case. Dash was a nervous wreck.

"We don't know a thing," he whispered, distraught. "What are we going to do? Where do we start?"

"It's not so bad," Agatha commented. "We have profiles of all the people involved: the producer, the two leading actors, and the director."

"Yes, but what are they involved in?"

Chandler cleared his throat. "Apparently they're making a film called *Fatal Error*," he summarized. "I saw the treatment among the case files—"

"What's a treatment?" Dash grumbled.

"It's Hollywood insider slang for a screenplay summary. A screenplay, of course, includes the whole plot of a movie, complete with all scene locations, dialogue, and action descriptions, right down to the camera angles," Agatha explained. She couldn't wait to dive in and read it. With a title like *Fatal Error*, it might have a mystery plot!

Dash tugged at his hair, as he always did when he was anxious. "But we don't know the most crucial thing," he said. "What crime was committed?"

Watson suddenly woke up inside his carrier and let out a yowl, making Dash jump.

"Relax, cousin," Agatha said, smiling. "If the producer, Robert Royce, hasn't revealed why he

called Eye International, it must mean that he wants to keep it as private as possible."

As always, her assumption was right on the money.

They landed at the crowded Los Angeles airport at 7:40 p.m. and went out the side exit. A tall, burly man was waiting for them at the curb, leaning on a sparkling red convertible. Agatha recognized him by his stature and dark, curly beard.

"Uncle Bud!" she shouted, waving a hand as she ran to meet him.

A smile lit up the stuntman's craggy face. "You've got to be Agatha!" he said in a booming voice as he lifted her up using only one arm. "And this handsome dude must be Dash!" he added, pulling Dash off the ground with his other arm.

Chandler stood a few paces behind with the luggage and Watson's cat carrier, watching in appreciative silence. He felt an instant rapport with this fellow strongman.

"So, you've decided to ditch foggy London for some California sun? Gonna catch a few rays on the beach?" Bud Mistery laughed.

"Actually, Uncle . . . ," Dash said through clenched teeth. "We're here about a rather tricky matter."

Agatha met his gaze, blushing. "I already let Uncle Bud know about the investigation," she admitted. "I hope you don't mind . . ."

Uncle Bud turned to Dash and saluted. "At your service, Agent DM14!" he announced solemnly. Then he grinned, adding, "Who would've guessed I'd have an ace detective for a nephew? That's fabulous!"

In spite of himself, Dash was flattered by the warm welcome. He turned his attention to the chrome trim and worn leather seats of the cherry-red car. It was bright and shiny, but the streamlined design and some well-disguised dents revealed its old age.

"She's a '59 Chevy Impala," said Bud Mistery, running his hand along the door. "The highlight of my collection!"

"Can we get going, Uncle?" Agatha urged him. "We're in a bit of a hurry!"

"No worries. Hop in!"

Within moments, Uncle Bud casually slipped onto the busy Pacific Coast Highway, lined on both sides by tall palm trees. They could still see

the sunset glow over the ocean. Bud whistled as he drove, the salty breeze riffling his hair. "So we're heading to the location you told me about on the phone? In Century City?" he asked.

"It's the office of producer Robert Royce," added Dash.

"Royce Pictures, I know it well," confirmed Bud. "I've done stunts on a few of his films. We'll be there in no time flat!"

He stepped on the gas and, spinning the steering wheel sharply, zigzagged from one lane to another, passing cars right and left.

"I hope we arrive in one piece," said Chandler, holding on to the door.

"Don't worry, pal," replied Bud, raising his voice over the roar of the engine. "I could drive this road blindfolded, if I had to!"

Half an hour later, the skyscrapers of Century City rose out of the darkness. The mirrored façades reflected nearby buildings

and the lights from passing cars.

"Here we are," said Bud, nodding toward one of the buildings. The silver plaque mounted on granite announced that the facility housed law firms, corporate consultants, and production offices. The Royce Pictures suite was on the twenty-second floor.

Robert Royce answered his own door with an air of impatience. With close-cropped hair and a square jaw, he looked like a man who always got what he wanted.

"Bud Mistery!" he exclaimed. "What are you doing here? You've put on a few pounds, hey?"

"Well, actually—"

"Look, if you're trying to hustle up work, drop me an email or call me tomorrow. I've got an important meeting lined up—"

"Mr. Royce?" Agatha interrupted, reaching to shake his hand. "We *are* your important meeting. Eye International sent us."

Cast of Characters

After looking them up and down with a visible frown, Royce invited them into his office. The oak-paneled walls were covered with autographed photos of film stars. Three people sat at the big conference table, and the producer hurried to introduce them.

Gerard Montgomery was the film's director. Short, overweight, and disheveled, he wore round, wire-rim glasses and barely made eye contact as he muttered a greeting. His mouth was set into a deep frown, and he stared at a silver-knobbed cane in his hands.

Alicia Prentiss was the star of the film. Her long blond hair was piled up high on her head. She had a vacant, distracted stare, as though she hadn't slept much the night before. Shaking off her torpor, she pasted on a smile and greeted them with an affected trill. "Hello, darlings!"

James Hill was the leading man. He had the swaggering air and charming smile of someone

who loves to be the center of attention. His hair was slicked back, and he wore a vintage double-breasted suit that showed off his muscular build. He greeted them with a self-important nod.

"So, Mr. Royce, tell us what happened," Agatha invited him.

The producer paced back and forth. "One month ago, we started filming *Fatal Error*," Royce told them. "It's a noir film set in the fifties, shot in black and white."

"A change of pace from most of the violent, vapid, special-effects epics everyone's making these days," grumbled Montgomery. "Everyone has forgotten the genius of Alfred Hitchcock and Orson Welles!"

"Calm down, Monty," Royce said. "Then the accidents started to happen—"

"What accidents?" Dash interrupted, on tenterhooks.

"I'm getting to that," replied Royce. "At first,

it was just little things. Klieg lights blowing, props disappearing, cameras jamming or rolling off track. Then people began to get hurt."

"You could say there were *fatal errors!*" Hill said with a snorting laugh.

Royce shot the actor an icy stare and continued. "We shot a scene where Alicia had to attack James with a knife with a retractable blade. Except someone replaced the stage knife with a real one, and James got hurt."

"It was so horrible, Jimmy," whimpered the blonde.

"Just a scratch, baby," replied Hill in a tough-guy voice.

"What did the police find out, Mr. Royce?" Agatha interrupted.

"We never told them," said the producer. "They would have shut down the production. The delays were already costing me buckets of money . . ."

"But what is money when you're making art? This film is going to elevate me to the level of Murnau and Lang!" rasped Montgomery.

Royce raised his voice and continued. "And now there's this new bit of trouble," he said, meeting the gaze of his stars. "Yesterday morning, James, Alicia, and Monty received these threats." He pulled three letters out of his desk drawer and laid them on the table.

Agatha examined them with her companions. The messages were pasted together with letters cut out of a newspaper, and each said exactly the same thing:

STOP THE FILM NOW, OR I'LL STOP YOU FOREVER.

"Do you have any suspects, Mr. Royce?" asked Agatha, her tone turning serious.

"One giant one," he replied drily.

"Someone on the crew?"

"Yeah, maybe this Lang or Murnau?" guessed Dash.

"You are an imbecile, boy!" shouted Montgomery, beating the knob of his cane on the table.

The young detective jumped back in fright.

"Dash, dear, pay no attention to his little rants," Alicia consoled him as Agatha sighed.

"Cousin, Fritz Lang and F. W. Murnau were two of history's greatest directors."

"Ah," Dash whispered, embarrassed. "Thank goodness for your memory drawers."

"As I was saying"—Royce cleared his throat—"I blame Saul Lowenthal."

"That fat cat?" Uncle Bud spoke up for the first time. Chandler echoed, "The famous producer?"

"Exactly," Royce said with confidence. "I scooped him on the screenplay for this movie, and Saul wants revenge!"

"How can you be so sure? The person responsible for these acts of sabotage would have to have access to the set," Agatha noted.

"Yeah, sure, but he could have hired someone," Royce answered. "An inside job. And that person must be on Saul Lowenthal's payroll. Get him and squeeze it out of him. If I know Saul, he'll tell you the truth just so he can brag about getting revenge on me . . ."

"All right, Mr. Royce," said Agatha to pacify him. "Where can we find Mr. Lowenthal?"

Robert Royce picked up a gold fountain pen and scrawled down an address. "Tomorrow night, we'll be shooting on location in the Hollywood Hills, so my talent needs to rest. If you want to find me, I'll be here in my office all day."

"We'll catch this Saul Lowenthal, sir," Dash assured him.

"If he's really the culprit," Agatha said under her breath as they left Royce's office.

The Walk of Fame

The next morning, after a good sleep and a delicious breakfast at Uncle Bud's bungalow, Agatha and her companions ventured onto the grid of streets that made up the Hollywood district.

As they walked, they realized just how impressive the city really was. It was an endless maze of streets, intersections, traffic lights, and unusual buildings, sizzling in the summer sun. They strolled past the Babylon Courtyard flanked by giant stone elephants, a wax museum, and a theater shaped like a Chinese pagoda. Tourists were everywhere, snapping photos and buying

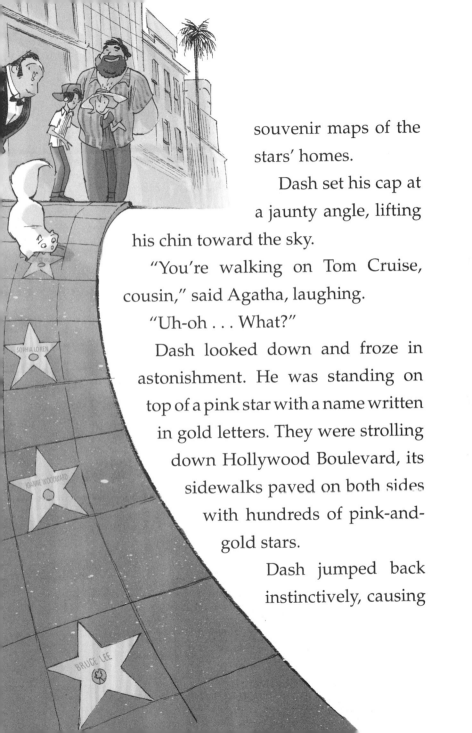

souvenir maps of the stars' homes.

Dash set his cap at a jaunty angle, lifting his chin toward the sky.

"You're walking on Tom Cruise, cousin," said Agatha, laughing.

"Uh-oh . . . What?"

Dash looked down and froze in astonishment. He was standing on top of a pink star with a name written in gold letters. They were strolling down Hollywood Boulevard, its sidewalks paved on both sides with hundreds of pink-and-gold stars.

Dash jumped back instinctively, causing

Chandler to use his boxer's reflexes to dodge out of his way.

"Um . . . why are there all these names on the sidewalk?"

"Don't you know about the Walk of Fame?" asked Agatha, stunned. "This is a tribute to all the most famous artists in music, TV, and film."

"Wow! Cool!" Dash walked along with his eyes glued to the ground. "Except I don't recognize any of these . . . Wait, no, there's Bruce Willis!"

"You might want to watch where you're going," snickered Agatha as Dash ran into one of the palm trees planted along the street.

Uncle Bud laughed and picked him up, dusting off his T-shirt with powerful hands.

"Ow! That hurt!" shrieked Dash, rubbing his nose. "This is why everyone says LA is a dangerous city!"

Watson, inside his cat carrier, looked amused,

then stretched out to sleep.

"How far is the Dolby Theatre?" asked Chandler, reminding everyone of their mission.

Uncle Bud pointed to a giant gold statue just down the street. "Right over there."

They followed him down the increasingly crowded street until they stood in front of the towering statue. Before they went into the theater, Dash stopped to examine it closely. "It looks like a giant Oscar statuette," he remarked.

"Exactly, dear cousin. Do you want me to give you some Hollywood history? The Academy Awards have been held in this very theater every year since 2002!" said Agatha, chuckling. "Picture the red carpet, right over there."

Dash stood blinking in silence. Then he exclaimed, "We have to take a picture. I want to give Oscar a hug. My friends won't believe their eyes!" He struck a pose, beaming. "Come on, take the picture!"

He had barely stopped talking when an angry security guard approached from behind. "No touching the statue," he growled. "I'm gonna kick you out."

"I'm sorry, I didn't know," Dash said nervously, backing away.

Just then, Uncle Bud spoke up. "Yo, Ernie, is my nephew giving you trouble?" he jokingly greeted the guard.

"Oh man, Bud, it's been way too long! You put on a few pounds, hey?" the guard answered. "What brings you to this tourist trap?"

"We need to speak to the boss, if you'll let us through . . ."

"He'll be inside screaming at someone, as usual! Go on . . . anything for LA's primo stuntman!"

Uncle Bud smiled at Agatha and urged Dash forward, laying a hand on his back. Escorted by Ernie, they entered the cavernous theater, passing under the archway that led to the seats.

The wide stage was packed with actors, singers, and dancers rehearsing a musical number. They were constantly interrupted by the comings and goings of technicians and crew members rolling in pieces of scenery.

"The boss is in the front row," whispered Ernie, indicating Lowenthal with a nod.

At that moment, everyone's attention was drawn to a woman with flaming red hair who stalked up the aisle with long strides. She passed by them without even a glance.

"She must have been arguing with someone," Agatha noted. "She looked furious."

"That's Jade Lombard," Uncle Bud informed them. "Lowenthal's latest young wife." He led them toward the producer, and Agatha noticed that even tough Ernie looked intimidated.

"Excuse me, Mr. Lowenthal?"

A heavyset man, who had a mustache that

looked like it had been drawn on with a pencil, was slouched in one of the seats. He held an unlit cigar in one hand and gesticulated wildly with the other as he shouted instructions at everyone. At Ernie's voice, he turned his head, ready to bark. Instead, he sat up in his chair with a grin.

"If it isn't Bud Mistery! What a surprise! Looking for work as a chorus boy?" he laughed.

"Not me, Saul . . ."

"That I believe," the producer interrupted. "You've put on a few pounds, am I right?"

"So they tell me," Bud said. "I'd like to introduce my niece and nephew."

Saul Lowenthal glanced at Agatha and Dash, sticking his unlit cigar back between his teeth. "I got nothing for them," he said, losing interest. "No kids in this show."

"Mr. Lowenthal," Agatha said. "We're not here to audition. Robert Royce sent us. We're conducting an investigation on his behalf."

Lowenthal stared at her, then burst into a laugh so loud, it sounded like an explosion. "HA-HA-HA! Is there nothing that con man won't try? Kiddie detectives! HA-HA-HA-HA!"

"Could we speak somewhere more private?" Agatha asked.

"Sure, kid. I need a smoke, anyway." Wending his way between actors and sets, Lowenthal led the group to a large courtyard. He lit his cigar with a silver lighter and look a long puff. "Go on, I'm all ears," he declared.

As Agatha detailed the reason for their visit, Lowenthal's expression went from jovial to outright amused.

"Royce is a moron," he declared when she finished. "Not to mention a no-talent hack."

"You certainly don't mince words," Chandler observed.

The producer's smile disappeared. "Look, I got no obligation to tell you a thing, but I'm going to tell you, anyway," he rumbled. "I never wanted to produce *Fatal Error*. It's going to be a total flop. Royce is obsessed with period films, but nobody wants to see that stuff anymore. To make matters worse, he's hired a has-been director and a cast of losers. That film's gonna go down in flames."

"So why did you try to buy the screenplay Royce wanted?" asked Dash, surprised.

"Just to show him that I had more clout. In Hollywood, money means nothing. It's your reputation that matters."

"So it's all about power," Agatha replied.

"Exactly. The big fish eats the little fish, and Royce is a guppy." Lowenthal chewed his cigar. "So I saddled him with a piece of garbage he thinks is a work of art." He laughed. "His loss."

"That doesn't seem very fair," said Dash.

"Hey, kid, if you want to run things, you have to act like a boss," he replied. "And don't you go thinking that Royce is a saint . . ."

"What do you mean?" asked Agatha.

"Did Mr. Honesty, Robert Royce, tell you the fast one that he pulled on Edwards?"

"Edwards?" asked Agatha, frowning.

"Waldo Edwards, the rookie who wrote *Fatal Error*. After he'd written six drafts of the screenplay, he found out he'd been working for free. HA-HA-HA-HA!"

The children exchanged puzzled looks, which didn't escape Lowenthal. "I can see you don't have a clue about showbiz!" he said smugly. He relit his cigar and went on. "Waldo writes books. It's his first produced screenplay, and Royce added a clause to his contract in confusing legal jargon. Just a little deceit in the fine print, saying that if anyone else rewrote his original screenplay, Edwards would not get paid."

"I suppose that's exactly what happened," guessed Agatha.

"You got it. So, as you can see, I'm not the only shark in this ocean," Lowenthal said with a devilish grin.

"Agatha, maybe this Waldo Edwards is our man!" whispered Dash.

"We can't rule it out," she replied softly. "He's got the perfect motive for wanting revenge on Royce." She met the producer's eyes. "Thank you, Mr. Lowenthal," she said, closing her

notebook. "Now could you please tell us how to contact Waldo Edwards?"

"I must have that hack's address somewhere," he said, scrolling his phone contacts. He scribbled it down and stomped back into the theater, shouting orders at everybody in sight.

Newspaper Clippings

The chrome trim on the Chevy Impala gleamed in the slanting, late afternoon light. "Where exactly are we going, Uncle?" asked Dash, stretching out in the backseat.

"This writer guy, Edwards, lives clear on the opposite side of LA. It'll take us a while to get there. But don't worry, kid—you've got me at the wheel."

As they zoomed down the Santa Monica Freeway, passing cars, vans, and trucks, Chandler started to cough. "I'm starting to feel nostalgic for London's clean air," he said sarcastically.

"I know what you mean," agreed Agatha,

rubbing her eyes. "If memory serves, Los Angeles is one of the most polluted cities in America. High mountains plus heavy traffic equals smog."

Dash raised his voice over the engine noise and said, "Let's review what we know so far about this investigation. What is your intuition telling you?"

"We'll have a much better idea once we speak to Edwards," said Agatha thoughtfully. She petted Watson, who was purring on her lap. "What strikes me is that Robert Royce didn't even mention that the screenwriter of *Fatal Error* might have a motive. It seems strange, since he told us about the sabotage and the threatening letters, but then steered us straight to a rival producer."

"I've got a bad feeling about this." Dash sounded worried. "Nobody has been murdered, sure, but those threats sounded serious . . ."

Agatha shot a quick glance at Uncle Bud,

as if inviting him to speak. After a moment, he said, "Dash is right on the money. We need to be very careful. LA is a beautiful city, with sunshine three hundred days a year, but it's got some dark shadows. Crime is everywhere here."

They all promised to keep their eyes open. Then Bud treated them to a California tradition, the In-N-Out Burger Double-Double with milk shakes and fries.

Waldo Edwards lived in a neighborhood where the houses were so similar that it was hard to tell one from another. The main street was crowded with Chinese restaurants, Korean newsstands, and Indian grocers, each with signs in two or more languages. Pizzerias and Mexican food trucks sprouted up here and there, but even Dash was too full to be tempted by street food.

They parked the car and walked past a cluster of young children playing in the street. One of them had opened a fire hydrant and was

laughing uproariously as he splashed passing cars. He laughed even harder when the jet of water hit Dash at full force. Dash muttered to himself, took a deep breath, and kept walking. Maybe his Sensei's Zen lessons were working.

Edwards's apartment building sat on the corner. They passed through a dark lobby and climbed up the first flight of stairs. The smell of paint indicated that the walls had recently been freshened up.

The apartment was on the top floor. Agatha knocked softly. There was no response from inside, but her knock caused the door to swing open a little.

"That's strange," she noted. "It's not locked."

Uncle Bud swung it open the rest of the way with a slight prod from his foot, like a cop in a Hollywood movie. The small apartment was dark. Faint rays of light filtered through

the venetian blinds, striping the walls with deep shadows.

Dash groped around for a light switch.

As soon as the lights flickered on, they saw two armchairs flanking a small glass-topped table. On top of it was a stack of newspapers, some of which had clearly been cut up. Other pages were spread on the floor, which was littered with scraps.

Agatha looked around the room. Tall wooden bookcases covered one wall. She shifted her gaze and noticed an old black Remington typewriter. It was obvious that Edwards didn't use a computer to write. At the back of the apartment was a small bedroom.

"Aha!" Dash exclaimed, pointing at the glass table. "We've caught the culprit!"

Agatha approached cautiously. She had the threatening letters with her and wanted to compare them with the cut-up newspapers.

"No doubt about it," she said after a minute. "These letters were cut out of these newspapers."

"And here are the tools," added Chandler, indicating a pair of scissors, a glue stick, and latex gloves hidden behind the typewriter.

"What did I tell you, cousin? Waldo Edwards is our man!" said Dash, satisfied. "Let's call Mr. Royce and tell him that the case is closed!"

"Our friend must have left in one heck of a hurry," Uncle Bud's booming voice called from the bedroom. "Come take a look!"

Agatha and Dash joined him. The closet was completely empty, as was the chest of drawers. A couple of T-shirts were strewn on the unmade bed, and a small suitcase sat open in the corner.

"We need to search the apartment," said Uncle Bud.

"I'm sure you know the drill, Uncle!" Agatha smiled at him.

"We're wasting time," Dash grumbled,

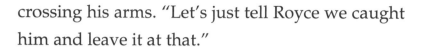

crossing his arms. "Let's just tell Royce we caught him and leave it at that."

Before he'd finished speaking, Agatha was back in the other room, riffling through Edwards's desk. Finding nothing suspicious, she went to inspect the bookcase. Her heart leapt to see that it was packed with mystery novels and thrillers. She noticed that they were all well-thumbed and faded. Maybe Edwards had bought them at thrift stores.

Then a thick hardcover caught her attention. Unlike the other books, it looked like it was fresh off the press. "Have you found something interesting, Miss Agatha?" asked Chandler curiously.

"Four Dead Bodies and a Brunette," replied Agatha, showing him the book. "By Waldo Edwards. He wrote it."

She turned the book over. The screenwriter's photo was on the back cover. He had small pale eyes that seemed to disappear behind thick-rimmed glasses. His limp blond hair was tied back in a long ponytail.

"Doesn't look like a tough guy," observed Uncle Bud, looking over her shoulder. "I wouldn't cast him as the criminal type."

"Let me see!" clamored Dash.

But just as he reached for the book, the lights went out suddenly. Two loud bangs and bright bursts of gunfire pierced the darkness.

"Hit the ground! He's got a gun!" yelled Uncle Bud.

A wild yowl filled the air as something flew toward the intruder.

Dash launched himself through the darkness.

"I've got him, I've got him!" he shouted.

"He's got me! He's got me!" cried Uncle Bud.

Agatha crouched under the desk, and Chandler blocked her with his own body. The yowls became louder.

"I've got him immobilized! The Python Grasp is working! Uncle, come help me!"

"I can't!" thundered Bud Mistery. "Some thug's got my legs!"

After a series of loud thumps and crashes, something made of glass hit the floor, shattering into a thousand pieces.

Agatha, whose eyes had adjusted to the dark, saw the intruder sneak out, slamming the door shut. She gathered her courage and lunged for the light switch.

The lights snapped back on. If her heart hadn't been thumping so hard, she would have burst out laughing at the scene that met her eyes.

Dash and Bud were stretched out on the floor.

Dash was clinging to their uncle's legs. His eyes were squeezed shut as he shouted, "I've got him! I've got him!"

Bud was trying to free himself by throwing kicks, but Dash's grip was too strong. "I'll fix you!" he yelled.

"Um . . . guys?" Agatha called out. "You might want to let go of each other."

Dash opened his eyes, and after a moment of shock, released his grip.

Uncle Bud couldn't believe it. "Nice work, nephew!" He laughed. "You've got some serious strength for a skinny kid!"

"Are you okay?" Agatha asked them.

Bud jumped up, nodding. Dash got up, too, saying, "All good, but that was hard work!"

Watson had jumped onto an armchair and licked his paw with enviable calm.

Chandler swung open the door. "Our attacker is gone," he informed them.

It was bad news, but they all breathed a sigh of relief. It had been a close call!

A Cat, a Redhead, and a Gun

"I'll catch that crook!" exclaimed Bud.

"Watch out, Uncle! He's got a gun!" Agatha warned him.

Undaunted, the stuntman ran down the hall, closely followed by Dash.

"No one in the stairwell," panted the boy. "He must be outside already."

In the courtyard below, they could hear shutters closing, doors being barred, and nervous voices. It was likely that the neighbors had heard gunshots and did not want to get involved, preferring to stay inside where it was safe. That didn't bode well for witnesses.

"What do we do now?" asked Dash, excited. "Should we search the neighborhood?"

Agatha took a few moments to think, tapping a finger on her nose. "No, I think it's best if we go back inside," she declared. "Maybe examining the bullets will give us a clue."

"We'll catch up with him sooner or later," declared Uncle Bud. "It's only a matter of time."

Inside the apartment, Chandler was sweeping up glass and plaster debris that had fallen from the ceiling.

"Uncle Bud, could you please take a look?" asked Agatha, looking upward.

Bud climbed onto a chair and, using a pen from Edwards's desk, began to tinker, examining the holes. Moments later, he showed Agatha the results of his efforts: two lumpy bullets.

"I bet you can tell me what caliber they are, right, Uncle Bud?" Agatha asked with a wink.

"They look like .38s," Bud Mistery said with a conspiratorial nod.

"Hey, guys, I can use the EyeNet to find out where they came from!" said Dash. He pulled his device from his pocket and scanned both bullets with the 3-D sensor. Within seconds, he had an analysis of the metal contents and probable maker. "Now I'll check the Eye International database to find out who bought them and where they were sold," he added enthusiastically.

But his efforts were met by a sad beep from the device, and a message saying NO MATCH FOUND.

"Maybe the damage caused by the impact made it impossible to match," Agatha offered. "But there are other elements to take into consideration . . ."

"Like what?" asked the others in chorus.

"For starters, the fact that our attacker fired into the ceiling," she said with an angelic smile. "So he only wanted to scare us."

"Whatever his reason, he'll be in big trouble when I get my hands on him," growled Bud.

Dash stopped pacing and spoke. "Let's recap," he said, concentrating hard. "So Edwards came back. Maybe he forgot something. He saw us and fired to scare us."

"I'm not so sure it was Edwards," objected Agatha.

"What more proof do you need—a signed confession?" Dash asked sarcastically.

"Exactly, Dash. That's about all that's missing."

"I don't get it."

"Think about it," said Agatha. "Isn't it obvious that the entire scene was constructed by someone? The newspaper clippings in full view, the emptied-out closet, the darkened apartment, the sudden attack. It's the perfect setup to make us think Waldo Edwards is guilty. But a real criminal wouldn't leave such obvious clues. Especially

not one who's read so many mysteries."

Dash's face fell. Maybe Agatha was right.

"Excellent reconstruction," agreed Uncle Bud. "But who else could it be?"

"I may have a clue," said Agatha, taking something from her pocket. "I found this inside his book right before we were attacked."

It was a photograph. Waldo Edwards, looking depressed, stood next to Gerard Montgomery, who leaned on his cane with a surly expression.

Beside them stood James Hill, flashing his leading-man smile, with one arm around the waist of a scantily dressed Alicia Prentiss and the other around a flaming redhead with a feline gaze. It didn't take much to identify her as Saul Lowenthal's wife, Jade Lombard, the woman they'd seen stalking angrily out of the Dolby Theatre that morning. In the background, a huge Ferris wheel lit up the night sky.

"That's Luna Park, the amusement park on the Santa Monica pier!" said Uncle Bud.

"Why is Lowenthal's wife in this picture?" asked Chandler, scratching his jaw.

"The big question is, what were they doing together?" Agatha said.

Scrambling sounds from the stairs interrupted their thoughts.

"Quick, Officer! They're still up there! I heard noises!" a voice shouted.

"It's the cops!" hissed Uncle Bud. "We've got to beat it!"

"He's right!" urged Agatha. "Run!"

"Why? We haven't done anything wrong!" Dash sounded surprised.

"Of course not, but if they find us here, we'll be dragged in for questioning and we won't be able to follow our leads," replied Agatha.

"Follow me, kids!" Bud bolted the door shut, shoving a heavy sofa in front to bar it. "Let's go out the fire escape!"

Chandler raised the venetian blinds as a piercing noise filled the courtyard.

"Sirens!" cried Dash as a storm of blows battered the door.

"Police! Open up, or we'll break down the door!"

Agatha launched herself onto the fire escape, closely followed by her uncle, her cousin, and Chandler.

They threw themselves headlong into a narrow back alley, then carefully made their way onto the street where Bud had parked the red Impala. A small crowd of onlookers had gathered in front of the building they had just left.

"Do as I do," said Agatha.

With slow, indifferent movements, she climbed into the car as if nothing had happened. The others followed her lead. Only Dash kept glancing nervously at the police.

Uncle Bud started the car and drove off at a casual pace, slipping past the Los Angeles Police Department vehicles with their flashing lights. Minutes later, the Impala was lost among hundreds of other cars traveling north on the freeway.

Dash let out an elated shout. "We got away!"

"Are we going to Royce's now, Agatha?" Uncle Bud asked, never taking his eyes off the road.

"I'd rather chat with Jade Lombard about that photo first. You seemed pretty close to her husband, Uncle Bud. Do you know where they live?" Agatha asked her.

"You bet! Lowenthal has a spectacular spread in Beverly Hills. I'm on it!" the stuntman said, beaming as he hit the gas.

"And Dash?" asked Agatha. "Can you track down her phone number, probably unlisted?"

Dash punched the EyeNet's buttons with lightning-fast fingers. A few seconds later, he had Jade's private number.

Agatha thanked him and turned to their uncle. "Since you're a family friend, could you call Ms. Lombard and make sure she's home?"

Bud wasted no time confirming that Jade Lombard would be glad to see them. "I could hear Saul barking at her in the background," he said with a smirk. "They're supposed to go to a benefit dinner tonight, but the nanny just quit,

and Jade has to stay home with their son."

A clever smile crossed Agatha's face. "Couldn't be better!" she said. "We get her and not him. Now we just need to make one last move . . ."

"Call Robert Royce at his office?" said Chandler, guessing her intentions.

"Exactly." She smiled, satisfied.

The producer was still hard at work, but he was about to leave for the night shoot in the Hollywood Hills. Agatha confirmed that they were shooting a chase scene on location, and that all the actors would be there at midnight.

Sounding pleased with herself, Agatha told Royce about their sensational discoveries at the screenwriter's apartment. She indicated that they were focusing their attention on Waldo Edwards. Dash looked astonished as she hung up, stroking Watson's soft fur.

"If you don't think Edwards did it, why did you tell Royce that he's our prime suspect?" he asked.

Agatha didn't answer.

"Agatha, are you listening?"

Still no answer.

"AGATHA!"

"Excuse me, Dash," she said, staring at something in her right hand. She raised it to show him. But evening was falling fast, and the fiery light of sunset made it impossible to see what she had in her hand.

"Did you find something interesting, Miss?" Chandler asked.

"It looks like a shred of black leather. It was caught between Watson's claws."

"A clue!" cried Dash. "But what does it mean?"

"It's obvious, cousin," said Agatha. "It means we have a way to identify our attacker."

"Do you mean to say that in all that chaos, Watson managed to scratch him?" Dash asked breathlessly. "Is that what those yowls were about?"

"Well done, Dash!" she replied. "I can see you're going to be a great detective!"

"You're too kind," said Dash, pompously buffing his fingernails on his shirt. "Sometimes I surprise even myself with my own genius."

Uncle Bud and Chandler could barely contain their laughter.

*L*owenthal's Spanish-style mansion in Beverly Hills was surrounded by an imposing wall, lined with avocado and lemon trees, and covered with a tumbling red bougainvillea vines. It was impossible to see inside.

Bud pulled up outside the wrought-iron gates. Each scrolling leaf was monogrammed with the producer's initials, *S* and *L*.

An armed guard with an agitated German shepherd on a leash stepped out from behind a century plant, indicating that they should turn around.

Agatha explained to the guard that they had

an appointment with Jade Lombard. The guard conferred with someone on an intercom, and they were granted entrance.

The two-story home resembled a Spanish palace, with wide verandas, tiled archways, and cream-colored stucco. A gardener was trimming the lawn by the pool.

The butler, waiting stiffly by the door, invited them to come in and make themselves comfortable. He and Chandler exchanged polite nods.

"Listen carefully, Dash," whispered Agatha. "Now we'll uncover the real culprit!"

"Why, is he hiding here?" Dash asked in surprise.

Agatha sighed and stepped over the threshold. The modern interior clashed with the classic façade. An interior designer had filled it with geometrical furniture, shiny tiles, and a white staircase leading to the upper level.

The garish abstract paintings hanging on every wall could cause a headache with a single glance.

The butler escorted them into an even more unusual room. The décor had an undersea theme: sofas shaped like shells, terra-cotta fish on pedestals, a carpet patterned to look like algae in motion. Tucked into a corner, Jade Lombard watched as a hyperactive two-year-old bounced off the furniture, desperately trying to ensure that he didn't break anything. She was still dressed in the magnificent black silk gown she'd chosen for the benefit she was no longer attending.

"Hi, Bud," she said without taking her eyes off the boy. "Are these the friends you told me about?"

The stuntman introduced the group, quickly running through their names. Only then did Jade Lombard turn to look at him.

"You know, Bud, you're getting a little chunky," she said.

"Yeah." Uncle Bud laughed. "So they keep telling me."

"No worries. That sofa that looks like the *Nautilus* is stronger than it looks," the lady of the house replied, looking from Bud to Chandler.

Agatha and her friends interpreted this as an invitation to sit down and explain their visit.

But Jade seemed distracted. "Do either of you kids babysit?" she asked in a pleading voice. "My son, Tommy, usually plays with his nanny at this time of day, and I have no idea how to calm him down . . ."

The little boy was chasing Watson around the algae carpet, laughing happily. Dodging and jumping, he slammed against a pedestal topped with a turtle. Chandler intervened a split second before it crashed to the floor.

With a meaningful nod from Agatha, the

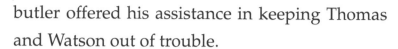

butler offered his assistance in keeping Thomas and Watson out of trouble.

"Thank you," Jade sighed, smoothing her fiery red hair. "Now, let's hear it."

Agatha pulled out the photo they'd found in Waldo Edwards's book, explaining what had happened in the vanished screenwriter's apartment a few hours before.

"So Waldo has disappeared?" murmured Jade, nervously munching a bunch of red grapes.

"So it would seem," replied Agatha. "We're trying to find out what happened to him."

Biting another grape, Jade said, "I don't know where Waldo is. Ever since he turned in the screenplay for that blasted film, he's been a wreck. Royce treated him like dirt."

"So you were the one who told your husband what Royce did to Waldo?" Agatha interrupted.

"I certainly did. Then Saul started spreading rumors to make Royce look bad, but it was poor Waldo who wound up being the laughingstock," Jade said bitterly.

"When was this photo taken?" asked Agatha.

"About a month ago. We met years ago on a set, back when I was still acting, and we've been friends ever since. On that particular night, I'd suggested we all meet at Luna Park to try to lift

Waldo's spirits. But it turned out to do just the opposite . . ."

"Why? What happened?" Dash asked.

Jade Lombard picked up a grape, glanced over to check on her son, and went on. "Monty—that's Gerard Montgomery's nickname—wanted to change the film's story to suit his artistic pretensions. Which meant Royce was able to exercise the clause he'd inserted into Waldo's contract saying he wouldn't get paid if someone else rewrote his screenplay."

"So Waldo might have a grudge against Monty—Mr. Montgomery?" Agatha asked.

"You bet! Waldo was ready to clobber him with his own cane. But the one they both hate is that skunk Robert Royce . . ."

"Why would a director hate the producer?" Dash interrupted. "Isn't Royce the person who hired him?"

Jade nodded. "But Royce wants to wrap the

film up as quickly as possible, and Monty likes to shoot each scene dozens of times. He claims it helps him achieve 'artistic integrity.' Every day on the set, Royce would harass Monty to speed it up, and Monty would refuse. That evening at Luna Park, all he could do was scream, 'Royce is trying to ruin my masterpiece! Just you wait, I'll ruin him!' Monty was furious. He's lucky he didn't fall off the pier, the way he was shaking his cane."

Uncle Bud leaned over. "You see, kids," he told Dash and Agatha. "Relationships in Hollywood are always tense. There's too much at stake: careers, image, money. Movies cost a fortune to make, and tempers get short."

"Plus everything in Hollywood moves as fast as possible," added Jade. "Monty is an old-school director, a thoughtful, fussy perfectionist. Royce accused him of being as slow to film as he is to walk, and that really offended him."

"So he uses the cane because he has to, not just to lend himself airs," observed Agatha.

"Unfortunately, yes," Jade said sadly. "Monty has a degenerative condition in his legs. It's very tiring. Even the cane won't help him for long, but he won't consider a wheelchair."

She offered the tray of fruit to her guests. Dash and Bud accepted, but Chandler was too busy tossing young Tommy into the air. He seemed to be having a ball.

"What else happened that evening?" asked Agatha.

"Well, Jimmy—James Hill— was cracking jokes left, right, and

center. He said he was trying to cheer Waldo up, but it seemed to make Waldo even more irritable. You know what actors are like. They have to be the center of attention."

Jade paused for a moment. "Jimmy's only had a career in comedy films. He's always got to get laughs. Unfortunately he hasn't realized yet that he's not funny, he's just ridiculous."

"Why was he cast as the leading man in *Fatal Error*?" asked Dash.

"Who knows? Maybe there's a tragic figure behind every clown . . . All I know is, Jimmy was thrilled because this film finally gave him a shot at a serious role. It was his big chance." She nibbled a slice of avocado. "But I also heard Royce wasn't happy with Jimmy's performance. He was even considering ditching him and recasting the role. At least that's what Monty told me that night, and he's not the sort to spread gossip."

"What a charming evening!" Dash added.

"Waldo was ready to punch Monty, but Alicia intervened, so he got angry at her instead. Not for the first time, I might add."

"Is Waldo a violent type?" asked Agatha.

"Not in the least. It's just that things are a bit . . . dramatic between Waldo and 'Alicia darling,'" said Jade. "They dated a long time ago when they were both starting out, but she dumped him. Waldo wasn't rich and powerful enough to do her any good, and probably never would be. Waldo's never forgiven her."

Uncle Bud shook his head. "I wouldn't have picked the lovely Alicia Prentiss as a social climber . . ."

"That's not all she is. She's also rude and insensitive. All night long, she kept making cracks about how naïve Waldo was to let Royce trick him into signing that contract without hiring an agent. She called him an idiot."

"I would have been mad at her, too!" yelled Bud.

Jade laughed. "As if 'Alicia darling' is any smarter in her business deals . . ."

"What do you mean?" Agatha asked.

"Alicia was offered a role in a much bigger film, so she begged Royce to let her leave *Fatal Error* before they started shooting. Royce just laughed in her face. She'd signed a contract with him, and he had no intention of letting her go. She would have earned five times as much from the other film as she would from Royce Pictures," Jade said. "So Alicia was furious. She called Royce all sorts of names. Then all of a sudden, something changed, and Royce became 'Robert darling' again."

"Hmm," murmured Agatha, tapping her nose. "Something definitely must have happened . . ."

"I'm sure, but whatever it was, I'm done with that two-faced witch," Jade said sourly.

"Then why did you invite her to Luna Park?" Dash asked.

"I did it for Waldo. I think the poor sap's still in love with her," the redhead replied.

"You care for Waldo a lot, don't you?" asked Agatha.

"Like a brother." Jade nodded.

"But you have no idea where he might have gone? To a friend or a relative?" Agatha asked.

"Waldo doesn't have any friends, and no family, either. He spends all his time writing books in that crummy hovel of an apartment. Of course he spends time with editors and people he works with, but then the book's finished and he's alone again. But he took a liking to Monty and Jimmy . . . maybe because they all love old movies." Jade took another bite of avocado. "Do you think you'll be able find him?" she asked, sounding worried.

"We'll do all we can," Agatha reassured her.

"And if you'll excuse us, we have to go now. Thank you for your help."

"Thanks for letting me vent a little," Jade replied. Then she scanned the room in search of her son and saw him curled up on the rug, fast asleep. "And thanks for your patience and child-wrangling skills, Chandler."

"My pleasure, ma'am," the butler replied with a nod.

A few minutes later they were back in Uncle Bud's red convertible.

"I've got another bad feeling," said Dash. "They all sound like spoiled brats. I'm afraid our investigation hasn't progressed at all after that gossip-fest."

"I wouldn't say that," replied Agatha, her eyes shining brightly. "On the contrary, dear friends. I know who the culprit must be!"

CHAPTER SEVEN
A Night
Shoot in Hollywood

"We need to get to the film set in the Hollywood Hills as soon as possible," Agatha urged them. "The saboteur could strike again at any moment!"

Uncle Bud backed up quickly and gunned the Chevy Impala like a rocket in the night. He accelerated so fast that Dash's cap blew right off his head, but the young detective was so deep in thought that he barely noticed.

"Do you really know who did it?" he asked Agatha hopefully.

"Yes, I do. I only have one nagging doubt, which I hope we can put to rest soon," she

mused, biting her lip. Then she started speaking at machine-gun speed. "I need you to do a search on your EyeNet. Try the archives of *The Hollywood Reporter* and *Variety*, the film industry trade papers, and search the name Alicia Prentiss."

"What am I looking for?" Dash asked, already typing her name.

"Her deal with Royce Pictures. Check her contract with the Screen Actors Guild."

Dash looked confused. "The Screen Actors what?"

Uncle Bud jumped in. "It's the union representing the legal interests of film and TV actors to keep employers from taking advantage of them," he said. "And since this is a company town, the trade papers love to report on who's getting paid what."

"Alicia Prentiss is a big star, so her deals will be newsworthy," Agatha added.

Dash quickly added SCREEN ACTORS GUILD

to his search, and the EyeNet sorted through hundreds of results at top speed.

"Oh wow!" he exclaimed. "Alicia Prentiss just inked a three-picture deal with Royce Pictures. They're paying her millions!"

"Perfect." Agatha nodded. "Just as I suspected."

"I don't see the connection, Miss," Chandler confessed.

"All will be revealed soon," Agatha promised. She looked out the window, lost in thought, as they sped through the night.

Uncle Bud navigated the uphill curves of a steep canyon road, climbing higher and higher till they reached a road at the top of the ridge with a breathtaking view of the city below.

"All right, here we are," he announced. "The *Fatal Error* set is just a stone's throw away!"

The Chevy turned onto Mulholland Drive, a cliff-clinging road that snaked over the rugged

A Night Shoot in Hollywood

Hollywood Hills. The veteran stunt driver clung to its curves until they reached an area blocked off for filming.

The night-lit film set looked like a world in chaos. Men and women from the crew bustled around, speaking rapidly into walkie-talkies. Several lighting technicians climbed up on high ladders, adjusting huge spotlights. The camera crew clustered around a rolling cart set onto tracks, testing its moves for an action shot. Agatha spotted two other cameras placed in strategic positions. There was a constant stream of managers ducking in to confer with Gerard Montgomery. Seated in his director's chair, the short man with the cane was shouting instructions and waving both hands.

Outside a star trailer a few yards away, Alicia checked herself in a mirror as the makeup artist, lipstick and foundation in hand, made a few finishing touches. Nearby, several mechanics

adjusted the tow rig on the car they would use for the chase scene.

Robert Royce stood alone by the side of the road, gazing down at the lights of the city. Maybe he was worried that Waldo Edwards was hiding amongst the cacti and shrubs, waiting to jump him. He startled when Agatha and the others approached him from behind.

"Sorry, I'm a bit nervous," he admitted, rubbing his temple. "This scene is essential to the film's plot . . . I'm just waiting for some sort of threat from that troublemaker," he said, looking at the group.

"Completely understandable, Mr. Royce," Agatha reassured him. "But we need to speak with you and the others in private before the next take."

Royce made a sharp gesture. Montgomery reluctantly pulled himself out of his chair and limped over, leaning on his cane and muttering

under his breath. Alicia swept over with a dramatic flourish, clutching the skirt of her 1940s diva gown to keep its hem out of the dust.

"Where the devil is Jimmy?" shouted Royce, turning to a skinny production assistant.

She pointed to the actor, who was examining a classic Packard with whitewall tires and tail fins.

Royce shouted at the top of his lungs, and James Hill strolled over to join the group. "So have you caught that crazy writer yet?" he asked. "Royce told us about that mess at his apartment. We're all worried Waldo might be lurking around somewhere."

Agatha looked into the eyes of each person in turn, as if she were reading their thoughts. Then she started to speak. "We haven't been entirely honest with you," she began. "We don't believe Waldo Edwards was responsible for the sabotage or the threatening letters. Actually we have reason to suspect it was one of you."

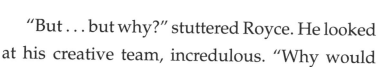

"But . . . but why?" stuttered Royce. He looked at his creative team, incredulous. "Why would any one of us do such things?"

"I'll explain that in a moment," Agatha promised. "But right now, I need you to show me your hands."

The suspects looked surprised and affronted. Dash, Chandler, and Uncle Bud stared at them in silence, trusting Agatha's intuition.

"Don't be ridiculous!" the director exclaimed, brandishing his cane. "This is downright offensive, little girl!"

"You can sound off as much as you like, Montgomery," Uncle Bud said, glaring. "But for now, be a good boy and show us your hands."

"Come on, Monty." Royce sighed. "Just go along with this nonsense and get it over with."

"Right now!" Dash commanded.

Alicia Prentiss held out her hands, palms down, and the rest of the group did the same.

"So, cousin?" asked Dash anxiously, chewing on his nails.

Agatha didn't respond. An eerie silence fell over the group.

"Can we get back to work now? Are you done wasting our time?" asked James Hill in a mocking tone, peering sidelong at Agatha.

Agatha gave a quick nod to Bud, who grabbed the actor's right arm and suddenly pulled up the sleeve of his jacket.

Poking out from a Band-Aid were three long red scratches. His black leather watchband was scarred.

"Aha!" Dash rejoiced. "You're the culprit!"

James Hill let out a sharp, nervous laugh. Then, with a quick twist, he pulled out a gun with his left hand and pointed it at Uncle Bud.

"Let go, pal," he growled.

Bud released his grip, raised both hands, and took a step backward, rejoining the others.

"Everybody stay calm and nobody gets hurt." James sounded more like a tough guy than he ever had on-screen. With a sneer on his face, he ran back to the Packard. He jumped in, started the motor, and screeched off before the stunned eyes of the cast and crew.

"Quick, Uncle! Follow that car!" cried Agatha, bounding into the Impala.

Dash and Chandler jumped in a split second before Uncle Bud took off in pursuit, the engine

roaring. "Hold on tight, we'll catch him!" he shouted.

"That ought to be easy," Dash said to his cousin. "That car is really old!"

"It's a show car from the set," Agatha said, her eyes fixed on the dark road ahead. "The body's antique, but it has a modern engine."

"I had no idea . . ." Dash sounded anxious.

The Impala sped over the hills like greased lightning. Dash clutched at his seat belt with one white-knuckled hand as they climbed higher and higher.

The tires screeched as Bud swerved around tight curves without losing speed. They skirted the steep sides, avoiding the lethal cliffs. The glow of Hollywood's lights in the valley below looked like a glittering tapestry.

"There he is!" yelled Chandler, pointing his finger.

The twin slash of the Packard's red taillights

appeared a hundred yards ahead, and then disappeared as it rounded another hairpin turn.

"We're right on top of him!" Dash cried out.

"Hold that thought!" Bud Mistery said, spinning the steering wheel like a NASCAR champion.

The Impala's engine roared, and Uncle Bud ate up the distance between it and the Packard until they were mere inches apart.

"Hold tight, guys!" Bud warned.

With sharp, sudden revs of the engine, the Impala started nudging the bumper of James Hill's Packard.

"Go, Uncle! Make him pull over!" yelled Agatha.

James Hill tried to escape Bud's maneuvers, but Bud was a pro. The final nudge made the actor's car lurch to the left so sharply that two of his wheels lifted off the ground.

"Got him!" yelled Uncle Bud.

CHAPTER SEVEN

The Impala slammed into the rear of the Packard. Hill's car spun around, coming to a crashing halt against a fence post. The windshield shattered into a thousand pieces.

The Impala slid into a skid. Bud spun the wheel to avoid the fence post, but the car plowed headlong into a concrete divider.

Silence fell over the Hollywood Hills.

The Hollywood Sign

*A*gatha looked around. She'd closed her eyes as they hit the divider, but the seat belt had saved her from harm.

They were in a large, open space with a few buildings, each with what looked like an enormous TV antenna.

Agatha looked over her shoulder. She saw Hill stagger out of the Packard and lurch away, his face bloodied.

"Ow! That was intense!" Dash moaned from the backseat.

Still a bit stunned, Uncle Bud jumped out of the Impala. The others followed.

"Quick, Uncle! He's getting away!" Agatha panted.

The actor was walking unsteadily. He reached the crest of the hill and vanished from sight, enveloped in a strange glow.

The group took off in hot pursuit. Just ahead, the word HOLLYWOOD stretched up forty-five feet into the sky, making Hill look tiny as he leaned against the base of the letter *L*.

"Give yourself up!" shouted Dash as he ran toward him.

"Wait, Dash! Be careful!" yelled Agatha, as the roar of another car engine grew nearer. From the corner of her eye, she saw a Cadillac skid to a halt beside the Impala. Royce, Alicia, and Montgomery jumped out.

Dash stopped in front of James Hill, who was clearly worn out, his face twisted in pain.

"It's all over, man," said the young detective, trying his best to look tough. "I'm Agent DM14.

Surrender this minute!"

But instead of obeying, the actor grabbed Dash by the collar. He pulled the boy in front of his body and held the gun up to his head. "It's not time for the closing credits just yet," he shouted to the others. "No tricks, or the boy gets it!"

Moving slowly, they all formed a circle around him.

"Let the kid go and face me like a man," growled Uncle Bud, clenching his fists. Chandler cracked his knuckles menacingly by his side.

Dash felt the cold metal of the gun press against his forehead. His head was throbbing, but he heard Sensei Miyazaki's words echo in his mind: *"Breathe, Lazy Squirrel, breathe . . . Concentrate and find your center . . ."*

The gun felt less cold, and the throbbing receded. Dash remembered the rope exercise, and imagined that everything was moving in slow motion. Even Hill's threatening voice seemed far

away, like something in a dream.

"Breathe, breathe . . ." he said aloud to himself.

He took a deep breath, releasing himself from his thoughts. Then, with a quick swivel, he managed to slip from Hill's grasp, stepping to one side and hitting the actor's wrist with a knifelike chop.

Hill dropped the gun, startled, and turned just in time to see Uncle Bud's fist hit his face like a speeding train. He collapsed at the foot of the sign.

"Smooth move, nephew!" Bud congratulated Dash with a bear hug. The rest of them circled around, complimenting him on the graceful spin he'd used to free himself.

"It's the Twisted Eel," bragged Dash. "There are only a few people in the whole world who've mastered it!"

Agatha took him aside, kissing him on the cheek. "That was very risky, Dash," she

whispered. "My heart was pounding like crazy—as if I had tachycardia!"

"Tachy-what?" he asked, dazed.

"Forget it." Agatha grinned. "We still have some cleaning up to do."

They all stood in the clearing. Except for the glowing white letters, the landscape was dark and deserted.

Royce was the first to speak. "Can you

explain?" he asked Agatha.

She wasted no time retelling the events of the attack at Waldo Edwards's apartment.

". . . and Watson launched himself at the intruder. It was only afterward that we realized that he had scratched the attacker, and picked up a scrap from his watchband . . ."

". . . which led us straight to the culprit!" Dash finished for her.

"That's it? The whole plot hinges on a *cat*?" snapped Montgomery, cranky as ever.

"No, Mr. Montgomery," Agatha continued. "I already knew that one of the four of you must be responsible, because you were the only ones who knew about our investigation, or that we were going to visit Saul Lowenthal the next morning."

"So James Hill was following us the whole time, is that right, Miss?" Chandler asked.

"Precisely. He knew Lowenthal would steer us toward Waldo Edwards. Just like his wife told

us, Lowenthal told everyone who would listen about Mr. Royce and his contract scam," she said.

"It wasn't a scam!" Royce tried to defend himself. "It was simply—"

"This isn't the time," Agatha told him. "So Hill knew we'd go to search Waldo's apartment. He'd already arranged every detail needed to frame the screenwriter, so he just had to make him disappear."

"But where's Waldo?" asked Alicia, alarmed.

"I suspect he's tied up somewhere. Maybe in a basement," said Agatha.

Royce shook his head in bewilderment. "How did you rule out Lowenthal?" he asked.

"Right after the attack, we called Jade— Ms. Lombard—who was home with her husband," Agatha explained. "And you couldn't have been the culprit, Mr. Royce, because we reached you at your office. Beverly Hills and Century City are both too far from Waldo's

apartment. So three suspects were eliminated on the basis of timing."

"Also," she went on, "our chat with Jade Lombard cleared Mr. Montgomery. Because of his unstable health, he walks with a cane, and the attacker who fired those shots moved with great speed."

"I'm as fit as a young man, you impertinent brat!" the director snapped.

"I have no doubt, Mr. Montgomery," Agatha reassured him.

"You surely had no reason to suspect me!" sniffed Alicia Prentiss.

Agatha nodded. "When Dash discovered your three-picture deal with Royce Pictures, I knew you had no interest in compromising the film, Ms. Prentiss. And so, by process of elimination, we knew James Hill was responsible. Watson's scratch only confirmed it."

"Precisely, cousin," Dash crowed, even

though he'd missed a good half of her speech while demonstrating the Twisted Eel to Chandler.

"I can't imagine why Jimmy would do this," Royce said bitterly.

"You'll have to ask him, isn't that right, Mr. Hill?" replied Agatha, turning to their prisoner.

The actor raised his head. His injuries from the accident and Bud's punch had wiped the leading-man grin off his face, replacing it with a sneer.

"You want to know why I did it?" he asked. "Simple! *Fatal Error* is my last chance to jump-start my career. I did it all so newspapers and bloggers around the world would create a publicity buzz. I'd be playing the lead in a film that was cursed, get it? Plagued by rumors of accidents on the set! With a vindictive screenwriter who threatened the cast. What better publicity to give me the fame I deserve?"

His rattled-off confession left them all

speechless. "Let's face it, this film's going to vanish without a trace. So I thought up the sabotage. I framed Waldo Edwards. I faked the threat letters. I knew that as soon as I started to leak out the rumors, people would be obsessed with the film *Fatal Error*. They'd come to see it in droves, and I'd be a legend! But now . . ." James Hill's boasting voice faltered. He looked suddenly older and sadder, resigned to his fate.

"Now we better call the police," suggested Dash.

"They're already here," said a voice from behind him.

Dash turned to see Uncle Bud pull out a distinctive, shiny Los Angeles Police Department badge. A split second later, he'd handcuffed James Hill while reciting, "You're under arrest. Anything you say or do from this moment can be used against you."

"Well done, Officer!" Agatha laughed, seeing

Dash's stunned expression. "And thanks for all your help with this investigation!"

"But . . . ," stammered Dash. "I don't get it. Is Uncle Bud playing a part? He's a stuntman—or is he?"

Uncle Bud shrugged. "I'm a Mistery."

Within moments, a squad of police cars arrived at the clearing, sirens screaming and lights flashing red like a scene in a movie. They arrested James Hill and hustled him into the back of a squad car. Hoping to lighten his sentence, the injured actor confessed where he'd hidden the screenwriter of *Fatal Error*.

Waldo Edwards was found locked up in the basement of the actor's beach house in Malibu, just as Agatha had imagined. He was freed within the hour; he'd been under heavy sedation and had absolutely no clue what had happened.

The mission was a great success.

But Dash wasn't gloating like usual. He kept pacing around the dented Impala, repeating, "So Uncle Bud's a police detective, and you kept it hidden from me this whole time?" His face was creased into a frown. "I've been working with someone who has the same job as me all along?"

"Not exactly," said Agatha vaguely. "It will make perfect sense very soon."

"She kept me in the dark, too," Chandler reassured Dash. "Miss Agatha only let me know during the flight, while you were asleep."

Dash glared. "You told him before me?"

Before Agatha could explain, Uncle Bud ambled over. He'd finished collecting statements and tying up the details of the investigation, and was whistling under his breath. "I'm ready to go back to the shadows," he said with a grin. "Back to being an ex–race-car driver and stuntman who likes to fix up vintage cars!"

"Go back to the shadows?" repeated Dash,

even more confused. "What do you mean by that?"

Bud shrugged. "I'm an undercover agent. I work incognito. I mostly deal with illegal trade, which obviously needs to remain a secret."

Dash's eyes widened, thrilled by this revelation. "That's so cool!" he exclaimed. "It did seem a bit weird that there was a Mistery with an ordinary job like 'stuntman'!"

This statement made everyone laugh.

As the laughter subsided, Dash turned back to Agatha. "You're not off the hook yet. Why didn't you tell me sooner? We could have solved this case in no time flat!"

Uncle Bud picked Dash up in his strong arms and dropped him into the battered convertible. "Agatha and I agreed that you'd be the lead detective on this case," he said with a grin. "This way all the credit belongs to you, Agent DM14. I saw you in action tonight. I'm very impressed,

and your teachers will be, too!"

Dash's face flushed with emotion. Chandler and Agatha were both beaming at him, but Watson just let out a disdainful meow.

"And now," said Agatha, "it's time for that fine old Hollywood tradition, the wrap party!"

"Great idea," agreed Uncle Bud. "I'll take you to all to a nice little place on the coast where they serve the best seafood in California."

They drove back through the Hollywood Hills at a leisurely pace. Uncle Bud navigated every tight curve with slow, smooth precision.

An hour later, they were sitting inside The Old Crab, a beachfront seafood restaurant with a pirate theme. A cabin boy with an eye patch took their order with a hook-shaped pen. The lantern light and solid wood walls gave the impression of dining in a ship's cabin.

"I always come to this joint when I need to relax," said Uncle Bud as they waited for their appetizers. "I like the warm, welcoming atmosphere. Life in LA can get pretty chaotic. Everyone's on the move every minute. There's never a moment's peace."

"So we noticed." Agatha nodded. "Especially those Hollywood film people. It seems like everyone is desperate to get rich and famous, whatever the cost."

"I must say, I prefer the quiet of my rhododendrons," said Chandler.

Dash, who'd been silent for a while, basking in the congratulatory messages his school had sent via the EyeNet, leaned back in his chair. "I feel right at home here in LA. It's the ideal city for a detective: investigations, shootings, car chases, undercover agents . . ."

"True. But a great detective never forgets a promise, you know," Agatha said.

Dash blinked. "What did I forget?"

"Didn't you say you were sorry to interrupt Chandler's anniversary celebration?" his cousin reminded him. "How are you going to make it up to him?"

"You're right," Dash muttered, embarrassed. Then he asked, "How can I repay you, Chandler? Is there something special you'd like?"

The Mistery House butler and jack-of-all-trades didn't blink. "A five-layer Sacher torte."

"Okay . . . a Soccer Tart. I'll ask the waiter to order one now. If they don't have them here, I'll check every restaurant and bakery on the wharf till I find one!"

Dash hurried over to talk to the cabin boy waiter. Then he rushed out of the restaurant, promising, "I'll be right back!" The others enjoyed their delicious prawns, roaring with laughter every time Dash reappeared at the door empty-handed.

Agatha

Girl of Mystery

Agatha's Next Mystery:
The Crime on the Norwegian Sea

The Investigation Begins...

$\mathcal{D}$ashiell Mistery was a lanky fourteen-year-old boy with the muscle tone of wet spaghetti. His long black hair always looked as if he'd just rolled out of bed, or off the couch where he often spent all morning sleeping. He stayed up till all hours every night tinkering with all the amazing high-tech devices in his penthouse on the top floor of London's Baker Palace. His friends had nicknamed Dash "Doctor Jekyll" because of his night-owl habits, which reminded them of a mad scientist locked away in his lab.

When he first heard the nickname, Dash laughed and tried to shrug it off. But there was no way to deny that everyone in the Mistery family was a little . . . well, odd. They were deeply eccentric people with unusual jobs, living in every corner of the globe. Dash had an unusual job of his own, which he kept well-hidden from almost everyone. With a few rare exceptions, nobody knew about his stunning success as a teenage detective!

Even his father, Edgar Allan Mistery, knew nothing about all the dangerous missions that Eye International Detective School had assigned to Dash, investigating thefts, kidnappings, and other crimes. Edgar had divorced Dash's mother a long time ago and remarried recently. When his ex-wife enrolled their son at the prestigious academy, Edgar had made Dash promise to study hard and ace all his tests so that someday he'd be the director of London's famous Scotland Yard. Then Edgar had burst out laughing, always a sign he was throwing down some kind of challenge. A former Olympic athlete, he was a very competitive man, and nothing made him as happy as winning.

Ever since then, Dash had struggled to do his best in his classes and on every investigation to which he was assigned. But not this week—he was about to go on a vacation! No high-pressure final exams, no unsolved mysteries lurking on the horizon. The aspiring detective had seven whole days of blissful relaxation ahead. There was only one hitch: He'd be spending this otherwise perfect week with his dad.

"Same old story whenever I see him," Dash grumbled, climbing the ladder to the high diving board. When he got to the top, he grabbed hold of both rails. The turquoise pool shimmered on Deck Twelve of the majestic ocean liner *King Arthur* as it plowed through tall waves off the Norwegian coast. Wherever he looked, the young detective saw water: the endless, foaming sea, the sun glinting off waves in a thousand broken reflections. The emerald-green fjords shone in the distance, with waterfalls plunging down from a great height. And way down below was that tiny square pool.

"What are you waiting for, Dash?" his father yelled from the side of the pool where he stood with his smartphone, ready to shoot yet another video clip of his son doing something he hated.

Tanned, fit, and boyish, Edgar still looked like the top athlete he'd been.

"Are you planning to lose every challenge?" he said with a mocking laugh. "I already beat you at swimming and holding your breath underwater. You're such a wimp!"

Dash gritted his teeth as he inched forward on the wobbly diving board. Why had he ever agreed to go on this cruise with his dad? He knew it would be unbearable.

Sun, fun, and endless free food, he reminded himself.

The best way to settle this once and for all was to prove to his father he wasn't a loser. So Dash took a deep breath, trying to fight back his fear of heights, and stepped to the edge of the diving board.

"Let's see what you've got!" Edgar Mistery

cackled. "Did you see what a big splash I made with my double back somersault? Try and beat *that*, if you can!"

"Yeah, right . . . This time I'll show you," Dash muttered without much conviction. He set his feet carefully at the edge and spread his arms wide for what he hoped would look like a magnificent swan dive. "I'm . . . um . . . almost ready!"

But something distracted him.

A crowd of onlookers stood next to the pool, cheering and catcalling. The only person missing was his father's new wife, Olympic speed-skating champion Kristi Linstrid. She sat under a large umbrella slathering sunscreen on little Ilse, the latest addition to the Mistery family. Dash's baby sister shared his blue eyes, his long legs—and his obsession with shiny high-tech devices. She had spotted his EyeNet in his unzipped sports bag, and was fooling around with its buttons.

"Oh no!" mumbled Dash. "If she turns it on, I'll be in big trouble. Good thing I encrypted the passcode."

The shiny prototype, designed to look like a trendy cell phone, was only available to students of Eye International. Hidden inside the EyeNet's titanium shell was a high-powered hard drive with a wealth of secret archives, online databases, and state-of-the-art apps to assist with investigations.

"Go, Dash! You rock!" cheered a group of teen girls on the edge of the pool. He peered down and blushed beet red as they waved and blew kisses at him.

"What a heartbreaker!" Edgar Mistery declared proudly. He turned to the noisy group of bikini-clad fans. "We're throwing a party for my son tonight. Want to come?"

The girls squealed happily, as though they'd been invited to a private party with a rock star.

Embarrassed, Dash covered his face with his hands. It was official: This was the most awkward vacation ever. All he'd wanted was to spend a few days away from his boring homework routine, and he'd bent over backward to get permission from his school . . . for *this*?

Tormented by these thoughts, Dash thought about giving up on Edgar's challenge. He could climb back down the ladder, join Kristi and Ilse, and stretch out on a deck chair, relaxing in peace. As he turned his gaze toward them, a scene unfolded as if in slow motion.

This is what he saw. The EyeNet started screeching and blinking like crazy, and little Ilse freaked out and flung it away. It flew through the air, clattering over the slippery tiles and sliding toward the pool.

Dash had been assigned a new mission, and his EyeNet was about to drown!

Without stopping to think, Dash launched himself off the diving board with a spectacular twist. He plunged into the water with perfect style and popped up the edge, resurfacing just in time to grab the EyeNet a split second before it hit the water.

"Got it!" Dash gasped.

He turned it on to make sure it was still

working. It was. He was so relieved that he didn't notice that everyone was gaping at him with their jaws dropped, amazed by his champion dive. The girls broke into cheers, but Dash had already shot out of the pool, grabbed his T-shirt and flip-flops, and charged off to find his cousin Agatha in the ship's library. He ran past the lifeguard and into the hall, dripping water all over the carpet, ignoring every one of the ship's many rules. He pressed the elevator button, his eyes never leaving the EyeNet's screen.

The message from Eye International wasted no words. He reread it twenty times:

AGENT DM14,
MANHUNT ON THE KING ARTHUR. CODE NAME: "OPERATION BISMARCK." DETAILS IN ATTACHED FILE. PROCEED WITH UTMOST URGENCY. PS: SORRY TO WRECK YOUR VACATION!

The elevator doors opened, and Dash

pushed in between the stunned passengers. Wreck his vacation? Not in the least! The boy breathed a sigh of relief. An investigation was the perfect way to escape from his dad.

CHAPTER ONE

Library at Sea

Aspiring writer Agatha Mistery had memorized every inch of the *King Arthur*. When the towering ship had first launched from the docks of Southampton a few years before, there had been hundreds of newspaper articles and television programs describing its elegant British design and state-of-the-art navigation systems.

Bigger than the *Titanic*, and powered by massive turbine engines, the *King Arthur* carried five thousand passengers and crew members on cruises all over the world. It boasted all of the usual tourist attractions, distributed over its sixteen decks: restaurants, cinemas, swimming pools and jacuzzis, fitness centers, a day spa, ballrooms, a casino, and luxury shops.

But Agatha had no interest in any of these entertainments. Wearing a classic beribboned white hat and a cool linen dress, she sat scribbling notes into her trusty notebook. From the moment they had set sail, she had been happily lost among the rare maritime books and ancient maps in the ship's library on Deck Six, a quiet place organized in the best Oxford tradition.

What a gold mine for mystery stories! Her imagination ran wild.

"What do you think about a dark creature from the abyss coming up to the surface to menace our heroes?" she whispered to Chandler. She was plotting a mystery novel set on a cruise ship lost in the icy waters of the Arctic Circle.

The smart, pretty twelve-year-old often found inspiration in the far-flung places she and Dash got to visit. Sailing along the Norwegian fjords evoked images of stark contrast: the striking beauty of the picturesque landscape and the terror of the high seas. She pointed to a dramatic painting of a giant tentacled creature, framed on the library's wall.

"They might think their ship has been seized by the legendary kraken," she went on, tapping the tip of her small, upturned nose.

Chandler approached the painting and bent his enormous ex-heavyweight frame to examine it closer. "Did you just say *kraken*, Miss Agatha?" he asked. "The giant squid from the Viking sagas?" Without waiting for her to answer, he rubbed his square jaw and observed, "It might seem a little implausible."

A brilliant smile lit the girl's face. "It's a 'red herring,' a plot device to raise the tension," she said with a nod. "Of course the kraken won't ever show up. It only exists in the characters' imaginations."

"Er, yes . . . well, of course." Chandler coughed.

The Mistery House butler and jack-of-all-trades adjusted his tie and petted Watson, who sat on his shoulders. Every so often, the white

Siberian cat raised his nose and immediately dropped it back down, mewing in protest. The ship was kept sparkling clean, and the scent of disinfectant bothered his sensitive nose.

"Oh no, I got lost in my story again!" Agatha laughed, checking her watch. "It's almost dinnertime, and we're supposed to join Uncle Edgar tonight at the welcome dinner."

Dash's dad was the brother of Agatha's own father, Simon Mistery. Along with his love of competitive sports, Edgar was fluent in dozens of languages. Always ready to change careers at the drop of a hat, he was just as impatient with marriage and had recently tied the knot for the third time. He had three children, one from each marriage. The oldest son was the Parisian painter Gaston, followed by Dash, and now Ilse. Edgar, Kristi, and Ilse had boarded that morning at the Norwegian port of Bergen, joining Agatha, Dash, and Chandler, who had set sail from England the previous day.

To be continued ...